FLOP-EARED MULE

Frank Kelso

This is a work of fiction. All the characters, events, and locations portrayed either are products of the author's imagination or used fictitiously.

Written by: Frank Kelso

Cover Photo: Liz Gunning

~~~~~~

~~~~~~

Contact the Author:

mailto:frankkelso@gulftel.com

http://www.frank-kelso.com

http://www.facebook.com/frank.kelso.author

~~~~~~

This publication is dedicated to my island princess. *Te amo.*

~~~~~~

Flop-eared Mule

"Sandy, leave them pickled eggs alone," the Star's barman shouted and flung a wet bar rag in my direction.

"After all the pay I pissed away in this place, you'd complain about a few eggs?" I asked.

"You and your flap-yap partner ain't bought a drink in here since the Bar-M let you two go back in September. I done spoke to the town marshal. You two ain't nothing but vagrants."

I eased out the side door and tossed my partner, Russell, two of the eggs I'd pinched from the bar's crock. "Ain't this a kick in the head? We ain't welcome in there no more."

Russell and me kinda look more like kin than partners; sandy brown hair, scraggly reddish-brown beard, six-feet tall, and rawboned. I'm so slim, Ma called me biscuit-butt 'cause my backside weren't no bigger than two hardtack biscuits nailed on a plank.

"We've 'bout wore out our welcome here. I'm a-getting tired of living this way." Russell's shambling walk came from too many hours in the saddle.

Townsfolk prattled about voting Eagle Flats the county seat of Wilbarger County, hoping it'd bring prosperity and, maybe, the railroad. I couldn't reckon why, when not even twenty-five people lived here. We meandered along the windblown main street, all of three blocks long.

Russell stopped at a horse trough to wash down the eggs. He jacked the handle of the cast-iron pump, cupped his hand, and drank. He pumped while I drank.

I grabbed my hat when a gust tugged it. "At least the water's free."

We moseyed toward the stables, hoping to find an odd job— any job.

Russell drawled in his soft-spoken way. "Think it's time to move on?" He raised his jacket collar against the wind's chill.

I weren't even cold 'til he lifted his collar. "Soon as we get cash to buy grub for the trail."

At Clem's store corner, the town marshal all but bowled us over from the other way.

"Why it's the two jaspers I've been hunting," he barked. "Time's up, boys. The saloon owner wants you gone. The liveryman wants fifteen dollars feed and board for your horses. If you're in town come morning, I'll arrest you for vagrancy and send you to the county jail for a stretch of hard time."

"Josh," I said, "You know without our saddles and horses we can't go nowhere. Hell, no ranchman hires a puncher without a saddle. Every ranchman nearby is hard put for the winter."

"Sandy, you ought to've skedaddled after the Bar-M turned you out. Folks expected more from you than becoming a lay-about loafer." Josh continued along the boardwalk before he called back over his shoulder, "Tomorrow." Tall and broad shouldered, Josh'd grown too old to work as a puncher, and after taking the town marshal's job, he added an old man's potbelly.

"There's another kick in the head." I checked my pockets for the makings of a smoke, knowing I had nothing but the longing for one. I leaned against the weathered, board-and-batten siding on Clem's general store before lifting my foot to catch my boot heel on the bottom edge.

Russell squatted and yanked up a stem of dry grass to stick in his mouth.

After a glance at Russell squatted there, I realized neither of us had bathed or shaved in over two weeks. Given how grungy he was, I must be a fright. No wonder they wanted us gone.

While we lazed there, Mr. Beasley drove up and tied his fancy buggy to a post across the street. As he waddled toward his bank's front door, he waved, called to someone down the street, and veered from our view.

"I heard tell a couple of drives went up to Kansas late this year. Think if we headed over to Fort Worth, we might find somebody in need of punchers?" Russell squinted up at me.

"Be a good idea if we had horses and saddles. Josh is right. We waited too dang long to move. That's my fault. Thought something'd turn up, and we'd not spend the winter riding line."

"Right now, riding a fence line and eating everyday sounds right fine."

I slapped his hat brim. "Thanks, pard. Just what I needed—another kick in the head."

"Why do you say that? What's it mean?"

"Ma washed my mouth with lye soap when she caught me saying cuss words. Instead of cussing out loud as I grew up, I'd say, 'ain't that a kick in the head.' It's a habit now."

"Think ol' Pete at the stable would take my hand-tooled Mexican saddle to settle our bill for the horses and give us a little grub money?"

"Asked him to buy mine last week. Beasley is squeezing him, just like the rest of the town. Pete's got no cash for the likes of us," I said.

Heavy boots clattered on the boardwalk moments before Josh stomped around the corner of Clem's store. "God looks out for fools—this must be your turn. You two get down to my office."

I stepped away when Josh reached for my arm. "Whoa! You said we had 'til morning."

"Don't make me put you in jail. Why I did it, I can't say, but I got you an offer for work."

"What kind of work?" Russell stood, his brow furrowed.

"Work that pays money, fool." Josh grabbed his arm. "And gets you two out of my town."

~~~~~~

The run down adobe calaboose used cottonwood logs for a viga roof topped with a layer of dried out sod. It'd be dry inside when it weren't raining. Josh swung the jailhouse door open to reveal Mr. Beasley in an unpainted, spindle-legged chair too small for his bulbous butt. The purple tinged scowl on his face set me to thinking his morning prunes hadn't done their job.

"Here's the deal, boys." Josh sat behind his desk and nodded at the banker. "Mr. Beasley has a package waiting in Fort Worth and needs somebody to fetch it here. I figured two weeks' work with a wagon."

Beasley heaved a for-all-I-care shrug before he nodded. He wore his black suit buttoned to the top with a starched collar and black string-tie cinched tight, which fit his pinched face scowl.

Slouched against the thick-planked jailhouse door, I raised an eyebrow at the seated men. "What's the pay? Who's buying the grub? Whose team and wagon?"

"Mr. Beasley's providing the team and wagon." Josh glanced at the banker. "He figures fifteen dollars for your time."

I wondered why Beasley ain't said a word before I looked at Josh. "No, thank you kindly. Even if *you* meant fifteen apiece, which I know *he* don't," I nodded at Beasley, "We'd still be flat broke when we got back an' paid our debts. Noticed you didn't figure the cost of two weeks grub over there and back."

"You only have to ride a wagon over and back. Don't have to walk or carry anything. Can't expect me to pay both of you." Beasley spit out "pay" like it burned his mouth.

It hadn't rained in so long that the sod roof had dried letting a steady drizzle of dust fall from the ceiling. Every surface in the jail and the puncheon floor had a coating of dust as fine as talc.

I took off my hat and made a show of dusting it. "I'd love to dicker with you, Mr. Beasley, but I've heard you remark all too often that your time is valuable. Well, so is ours."

"Don't get uppity, Sandy." Josh jerked his thumb at the barred cells. "I could start that vagrancy sentence anytime you're ready."

"Say, that sounds pretty good, don't it, Russell? We ain't had a square meal in a week. You can put us up for the next week if you provide meals from Miss Betty's Café."

"I've had enough of your impertinence you … you …

puncher." Beasley's tongue slid back and forth across his front teeth, as if he needed to scrape off the word's bad taste.

"Might be a lowly cowpuncher to you, but I know my worth. You want your package fetched, it's fifteen dollars each, plus fifteen for food, plus five for a night's food, lodging, and to stable the team in Fort Worth, plus ten each for our rifles from your man at Clem's store—"

"Stop with the pluses!" Beasley's face shaded crimson. "Why should I pay for your room in Fort Worth? Why should I sell back your rifles? You aren't worth it—not hardly."

"Russell, what you want for supper?" I crossed to a cell and yanked open a heavy door that screeched in protest.

Russell's gaze flitted between the open cell door and the open door leading outside.

"Sandy, be reasonable." Josh rolled his palms outward. "It's an easy wagon ride over to Fort Worth and back."

"Bull. We both know a bunch of northern Cheyenne done busted off their reservation up in the Nations. They've been raiding south of the Red River 'tween here and Fort Worth."

"Ain't no Cheyenne in Fort Worth." Josh waved a hand as if batting flies.

"Maybe—but you want a dirty job done, and there ain't nobody else for it." I stepped behind the iron bars. "Add a sweetener or I'll stay here at the county's expense."

Beasley struggled up from his chair, snarling and snapping like a rabid dog, while he tried to find words to fit his anger. "Lock them up and give me the key." He waggled a finger at Josh. "I'm fed up with people hereabouts who think they can take my money with no consequences."

Josh guided the banker toward the open jailhouse door. "Calm down, Mr. Beasley. Let me work on this." He patted the older man's back. "I know what you want. I'll see it gets done."

The banker continued to gripe and complain as Josh closed the unpainted wood-planked door.

Face redder than his bandana, Josh stomped to his desk. "Ain't nobody else offering two punchers a job, and you argued with him, you dolt. This is how it'll be: You two will run this errand for seventy dollars or I'll carry you to the county jail tonight—and forget about any supper."

I shook my head. "Seventy still don't cover the cost of our—"

"You ain't listening. This ain't no poker game, where you just keep raising. This is the jail! You do it, or I'll lock that cell door and give Beasley the key. I'll leave for Fort Worth, and we'll see who's alive in here when I get back."

As I readied a snappy answer, Russell punched my arm. "This ain't no time to smart ass."

"I only wanted to ask if we could ride our horses—"

"Hell no! I let you two have horses and saddles, that'll be the last I see of you." Josh jerked open a desk drawer and snatched up a bottle. He swallowed a swig and then sighed. "I'll give you enough money to buy two weeks of food, get your rifles, and a little pocket money for Fort Worth. When you return, I'll get your horses and give you the rest when you ride out of town."

I smiled at Russell. "Give us the money. We'll get grub an—"

"Nice try." Josh guzzled another swig. "I'll walk you two over to Clem's to get back your rifles and buy some trail food. Keep in mind, the cost of food comes out of your end, so spend as much as you want—there won't be no more."

"So if we only buy dry beans, salt pork, and hardtack, you don't care?" Russell asked.

"Show you that my heart's in the right place," Josh said, "I'll buy you a beer at the Star, so you can eat supper at their serving tray. Have something more than the eggs you been stealing."

I glanced over quick to see if he hid a sly smile. "Being right friendly all of a sudden."

"Nah. It's cheaper than buying two suppers at the town's expense. I'll lock you in overnight, so you'll be ready to ride at first light. Beasley'll bring the wagon here for you."

~~~~~~

I slept good, considering where I bunked. When Josh opened the cell, I stood before I offered a couple of hard-boiled eggs to Russell, but he'd swiped two of his own.

Dang, we've sunk low. Sucking eggs like stray hounds.

After stepping outside the old adobe, I said, "You never told us what the package is. Where do we find it?"

Josh checked his boots. "Wouldn't have told you before. A coffin is waiting at the Tarrant County Sheriff's office. Some rank sidewinder robbed and killed Beasley's son six months ago. The old banker swore he'd see the man hung; he posted a reward—dead or alive. The sidewinder got killed in a card game shoot-out somewhere in the Nations last week. A drifter brung in the body and claimed the reward. Beasley intends to hang the side-winder and post the picture in the Fort Worth newspaper notifying all of Texas what happens if you mess with him or his kin."

Josh scratched the back of his neck. "Beasley ain't been thinking right since his boy died. I hope this ends his grieving. He has to stop treating people so mean. If he don't, he'll get bushwhacked one day after foreclosing on some piddling debt." He spat in the dusty street.

Russell gaped, open-mouthed. Bits of egg yolk clung to his moustache. "You're hanging a ... a dead man?"

"What'd we get into?" A shiver shook me. "I ain't right sure I want to fetch a dead man."

Russell's shoulders drooped as his back slumped. "Don't like hanging a dead man. It's bad luck—the worst kind."

Josh laughed at our worries. "I thought you two was rough and ready punchers. It's only a pine box you're toting. Ain't asking you to hang him, but I am ordering you to go get that coffin and carry it here. We've talked long enough. Mount that wagon and get on down the trail. I expect you back here in two weeks—no dawdling."

Don't know where my mind hid out, but when I spun on my heels toward the wagon, I gasped. "That ain't no team—it's only a flop-eared mule." The mousey brown mule resembled a much larger version of its ancestor, the lowly Mexican burro, and equally dusty and shaggy.

I slapped the rotted side of the small farm wagon, not much bigger than a buckboard. "This termite riddled rig won't make it to Fort Worth, let alone back again. Even if that sorry mule worked up a trot, this piece of crap will fall apart on the trail. We can darn-near walk faster than this rig can go."

In the back of my mind, I recalled tales about muleskinners. A sure sign of a cantankerous mule is a "flop ear," whose ear has been twisted for being stubborn and not pulling its load.

"It ain't what I expected either." Josh wagged his head and

dropped his gaze. "You get that coffin here soon as you can, and I'll get the store owners to add a few dollars to your pot."

Russell's face sagged like old, worn-out, hunting dog. You'd almost think they planned to hang him.

I slapped him on the back. "Let's get it done, so we can shuck this loco town."

He shook his head so hard his upper body swayed side-to-side. "Sandy, I'll do this to dig out of our fix, but this rips it apart. I'm heading home to Indiana when we're done."

"Indiana? I never knew you hailed from there. I supposed you a true Texan. All this time punching cows, and you never said." I dragged myself into the wagon seat.

"You never stopped talking long enough for me say." Russell mounted next to me.

Josh tossed two blankets from the jail into the wagon. "I'll see y'all in two weeks, hear."

~~~~~~

A man couldn't have a colder or more boring job than riding a fence line in winter, unless he drove a rickety farm wagon across north Texas to fetch a dead body. Russell has done dried up; he wouldn't talk, hardly ate, only helped hitching and unhitching that danged, ornery mule.

Two days before we reached Fort Worth, a snowstorm blew

up—a real Blue Norther—and it was a month 'til Christmas. The north wind had turned our lips blue the evening we rolled into Fort Worth. As we passed the square, Russell pointed to a courthouse sign—County Sheriff's Office.

"Hell no. The hotel has a bathhouse inside. I'm gonna get warm."

Russell nodded; cold had slowed his motions. "Yeah, warm." His first words in three days.

~~~~~~

Over a sizzling beefsteak in a stockman's café, I got to feeling human again after a bath and wearing china-man-washed clothes. I tried sitting quiet to get Russell to talk, but I couldn't hold it. "After a week on the trail, nothing beats a hearty steak supper for two hungry punchers."

"Anything's better than your dang beans." Russell's lips curled in disgust.

"My beans? You're the one who said he likes his beans burnt on the bottom."

We glared at one another before I grinned, and we both busted into laughter.

~~~~~~

The next morning, we ate a hot breakfast and then walked to the livery to hitch the wagon and collect our sorry load. The one-armed liveryman had the flop-eared mule standing outside. "Hitch your wagon and get this danged beast out of my barn." He swatted the mule's flop-ear with his hat and got nipped in return. "See? This is the orneriest critter ever. Get him gone!" He grabbed his overnight fee and stomped off cursing his bad luck, or maybe cursing ours.

~~~~~~

We drove to the Tarrant County Sheriff's Office. A deputy led us to a funeral parlor where we loaded the coffin. We rolled out of town at a funeral walk. The old mule decided he'd step no faster than he wanted.

"I can walk faster than this. Stop by those willows, and I'll cut some switches." Russell pulled his boot knife.

"You hop down. I'll keep him moving."

Russell returned with an armful of long switches. That ornery mule caught sight of him and broke into a trot. Russell, running to catch up, dropped about half of his load. Flop-ear slowed after Russell jumped on, but the mule moved faster than before. None of us liked the cold.

As we travelled northwest the next day, snow still covered the ground. We suffered another cold night. The mule grew meaner with each passing day. He snapped at us whenever we got within his range and kicked at every little noise.

"That mule is more temperamental than that red-headed saloon gal you wanted to marry," Russell said.

"Clarisse weren't temperamental. She was an *artiste* and you know they're high-strung." What bothered me most about Russell's comment was the mule snapped at people nearby just like Clarisse did. She'd often pout and get cranky when she didn't get her way. If I could just figure out what's got that flop-eared mule cranky, likely, I'd find some way to soothe him.

The next day dawned gray and bitter cold. As we rolled from a creek bed about noon, the mule stopped and perked both ears forward. I whacked him with a switch twice before he eased forward a step. If I hadn't been so cold, and the mule hadn't been so temperamental, I might have paid more attention before we rolled into some heavy brush along both sides of the road.

"Russell, move easy, but get your rifle ready," I whispered.

"I see them. I can't tell one from another." He leaned forward. "That them Cheyenne?"

Even if the mule wanted to break into a brisk trot, he couldn't have. They had us boxed within the thicket lining the road. I popped the reins across his rump to move toward them and slipped out my Colt Lightning, setting it on the wagon seat next to my leg.

Three Cheyenne blocked our trail. A big hawk-nosed man in

the center wore a trade blanket around his shoulders, but no shirt. A Springfield Trapdoor rifle lay in the crook of his left arm. He lifted his right hand to his mouth twice before he said, "Food."

"Give him something from the grub box," I whispered.

Russell tossed a can of stewed tomatoes underhanded toward the big Indian.

Hawk-nose caught the can. He eyed it with a growling grimace before he threw it at Russell.

"Give him the pork-belly," I said. "Do it quick."

The big Cheyenne caught the short slab of pork and tossed it to one of the others. He raised his rifle over his head, snarled angry words, wheeled his horse, and then they rode away.

I'd missed the Indian Wars in Texas. They'd ended by the time I'd growed big enough to fight, but I just learned I hadn't missed a dang thing. The mule added his two-cents; he refused to budge. Russell and I got out front and pulled on his harness. We kept clear of the mule's snapping teeth, and tugged until he eased along the brush-lined trail.

When we rolled out of the brushy area, I elbowed Russell. "You remember the old *segundo* telling about his days riding for the Texas Rangers? He told us most Plains Indians would eat a mule before eating a horse or a cow. Think they'll try stealing this ornery mule?"

22

"If they'll take that coffin with them, they can have him."

I laughed, but I knew Russell wanted to dump that coffin.

After supper—half of the can of tomatoes— I drew the first watch. Russell relieved me at midnight, saying he'd wake me at four. Instead, a heavy thump woke me. I thought it were a cattle stampede, but 'twas only one ornery mule stomping and kicking.

We raced to rescue the mule, but soon ducked for the ground. Flop-ear whirled in circles, biting or kicking from whichever end he could bring to bear. After we got him settled, we led him back to the wagon, only to discover our blankets and food stolen, and the coffin opened.

Russell's eyes grew bigger than a hoot owl's. "I told you, it's bad luck to move a coffin."

"Let's get hitched and start rolling," I said. "The quicker it's done, the sooner we're gone."

That danged flop-eared mule didn't agree; he refused to cooperate, again. I resorted to fitting a lip-twitch over his upper lip to control him. Russell struggled with the twitch to hold him still while I fastened the harnesses. We rolled out as the sky brightened for another bitter, cold dawn.

The sun came out by midmorning, but the day didn't warm. In the distance, the trail passed through a grove of cottonwood trees. The closer we rolled, the slower Flop-ear moved.

"All right, I get your message. You think them Cheyenne want you for dinner." As Russell and I debated about a way around an ambush in that grove, a Cheyenne sneaked up from behind.

Russell spotted the bushwhacker drawing an arrow in his bow and dropped him with a quick rifle shot. After Russell fired, the other two galloped from the trees, firing their rifles.

Flop-ear decided to charge them. I grabbed the seat back with one hand and fired my Colt as they raced closer. The two Cheyenne split one to each side as we passed. Russell spilled one rider by shooting his horse. Flop-ear stayed at a brisk trot for an hour before his panic settled.

The wagon grew noisier during the mule's fast trot, but I didn't waste no time finding its cause. When we stopped, I noticed the rotted left side had collapsed and the left wheel dragged—wouldn't roll. If we hadn't stopped, the back axle might've broke off the wagon.

"We got to leave that thing," Russell kicked the wheel. "I'd sooner fight them Cheyenne barehanded than ride with that accurse-ed coffin. Let's toss it and ride for Fort Worth."

"We're only two days out of Eagle Flats. Stay with me. We can do this."

Russell shivered head-to-toe, but not from the cold. "How we going to carry that casket?"

"Let's try to patch the wagon together." We needed three or four planks and some nails. I got busy cussing our bad luck, when I noticed the lid had popped loose from the coffin again. *There lays our lumber and nails.* I explained my idea to Russell.

"It just keeps getting worse. I won't touch none of it." Russell turned away.

"I'll knock it apart with my pistol butt. You drive the nails back through with yours."

I climbed into the wagon, tossed the coffin's slated lid on the ground, and knocked more pine slats from the coffin's sides. Thankfully, the body lay in a shroud, or I'd have lost Russell to the Looney bin if he'd caught a glimpse of the dead body.

Russell held the pine slats while I nailed them in place to reinforce the broken axle carriage. The nails fell too short to pass through both boards and bent over to clinch tight on the backside, but I hoped it'd hold 'til we got to town.

The brief rest let Flop-ear recover some of his orneriness. Russell grabbed the lip-twitch, but when he tried to grab Flop-ear's upper lip, the contrary mule sidestepped him and pulled the wagon. Russell leapt onboard as the wagon passed, his gaze avoiding the shrouded corpse.

~~~~~~

Near sunset, I searched for a place to camp for the night. A washout crossed the trail ahead. It had steep sides, but I reckoned the wagon ought to roll through. As we came up the washout's far side, the wagon's rear axle carriage broke off. The noise and sharp jolt spooked Flop-ear. He broke into a trot before I got him stopped. The wagon's tail bumped along the rough ground, causing the coffin's wood base to slide off, which let the shrouded body to roll free.

Russell leapt up and fired his Winchester repeater several times toward the body.

I slapped his shoulder. "What the hell are you doing?"

"Scaring off his ghost. If he ain't buried right off, his ghost is free to haunt."

To steady him, I grabbed his arm. "Russell, it's okay. We left his ghost in Fort Worth when they didn't bury him—ain't no ghost here now. Hold that danged mule, so he don't run off."

The axle carriage with the wheels and axle lay in the washout along with six loose slats. There'd be no repairing this mess. I pondered using the remaining bed like dragging a travois.

As I plod to the corpse, its shroud dusty and torn, I figured I'd use the coffin's wood base to drag the shrouded body over to the slanted wagon bed by myself. Russell would be useless.

After I tied the body and coffin base to the slanted bed with the brake rope, I stood on the seat and surveyed the area in the fading light. The wash, which broke the axle, joined the larger streambed below. A tall, dead tree leaned against the stream's steep bank a few hundred yards ahead. I reckoned that bank might be a dry place to camp sheltered from the cold wind.

Flop-ear dragged the travois to the dead tree, where Russell and I removed his harnesses. Russell slid down the bank to get a fire started. The mule couldn't slide down the steep bank, so I used the long reins to lead Flop-ear to the wash, where we eased our way down to the streambed. Enough dry grass remained beside the stream to feed Flop-ear. I let him drink the icy water.

I stepped close to pull him from the water. He dropped his head, gave me a walleyed stare, and kicked. His hoof came within a whisker of my head. I kicked his rear haunch in return. The mule brayed and snapped at me a time or two, 'til I tied his night hobble. All the time, I cussed him aloud, and then I stepped back to laugh as I tried to figure which of us was the real jackass.

Back in camp, Russell had a small fire banked against a ring of river stone.

"We'll warm up for a while with that fire, but let it die out," I said. "I fear the Cheyenne might make another run at us tonight. You take first watch. Wake me at midnight. Sit up top, beside the dead tree. You'll have a better chance of spotting them."

Russell hung his head and moped like a beaten dog. If he had a tail, it would've drooped.

~~~~~~

A rifle shot woke me. As I stood with my old .44-Henry, a Cheyenne hurtled from the bank and knocked me down. While we wrestled on the ground, I pulled my Colt Lightning and fired two quick shots, not aiming, just shooting into his body.

I got lucky; he jerked twice and lay still.

I scrambled up to help Russell.

"I got the other one," he whispered as I neared.

"Wahoo! Are we tough Texas hombres or what?"

Russell held out a worn envelope. "This here is Ma's address. Send me home."

"What are you—"

Russell sagged into me. I grabbed to hold him up, but I gripped the arrow in his back. I settled him on my lap as I sat on the ground. Russell grew cold in my arms while I cried.

At first light, I laid him against last night's fire rock and piled more rock on him. I had no way to protect his body, except the rocks, until I could return with another wagon to bring him home.

I hunted the area, but I failed to find the Cheyenne Russell had plugged or their horses. Worse yet, with all the shooting, Flop-ear broke his hobbles and wandered off.

I hated to think it, but without the sidewinder's body, the whole trip had been for naught. I'd not let Russell die for nothing. I had to deliver that body.

I set off dragging the coffin's wood-planked base like a sled with the brake rope. I grabbed the lip-twitch from the wagon's seat and set out tracking that cantankerous mule.

The track's directions had him headed for the barn back in Eagle Flats. As I followed him, I cussed that danged Flop-ear with every step. I found him about noon, his long wagon reins tangled in some brush. Being stuck and unable to pull loose had got him as mad and frustrated as me. He snapped and kicked while squealing like a fresh-castrated pig. Dang fool me, I cussed and kicked right back as I moved past him to loosen his reins.

A wailing banshee sprang from the brush. Hawk-nose, the last Cheyenne—wounded and angry—charged at me, determined to take my scalp and eat that flop-eared mule. If that crazy Cheyenne had agreed to eat the mule first, I'd helped him at that moment.

My only luck on the whole trip came when Hawk-nose attacked with a knife in his un-injured left hand. From reflex, I blocked with my Henry as he stabbed. Instead of ripping out my guts, his cheap, trade knife struck my rifle's brass receiver and snapped. I slammed his head with the Henry's butt before I reversed it to shoot him as he lunged at me. His dead weight carried me off my feet. I sat there dazed—amazed to be alive.

Flop-ear leaned down and bit the Cheyenne's ass!

I couldn't get past Russell dying and wiped my eyes. Untying the shrouded body from the coffin's base, I draped the body over the mule's shoulders before tying it to his wagon collar.

"See how you like that, you ornery SOB." I slapped his rump.

If I hadn't been so befuddled over Russell dying, and angry at this contemptible critter, I might have taken a warning from his loco antics that something else had gone wrong.

"Yup, maybe I'll notice your warning—next time."

I untied the long reins the big Cheyenne had used to hold the mule while he lured me in close. Flop-ear yanked away as soon as the knot came undone. His tug caused me to drop one rein, but I held fast to the other.

After I jerked him to a stop with the long leather strap I held, I bent to gather the dropped rein from the ground.

Once I'd bent down for the loose rein, it dawned on me that Flop-ear stood ass-end toward me—and way too close!

From ground level, I glanced across while Flop-ear lowered his head and sent me his walleyed stare.

Here's another kick in the . . .

www.ingramcontent.com/pod-product-compliance
Lightning Source LLC
Chambersburg PA
CBHW020323150626
46552CB00022B/3181